All About Worl...

Young

Keith Goodman

Published by G-L-R (Great Little Read)

Written by Keith Goodman

Reading Age for this book: 7+

The reading age for the series starts at seven

The English Reading Tree Series has been written for children aged seven and over. It is the perfect tool for parents to get their children into the habit of reading.

This book has been created to entertain and educate young minds and is packed with information and trivia, and lots of authentic images that bring the topic alive.

TABLE OF CONTENTS

Introduction

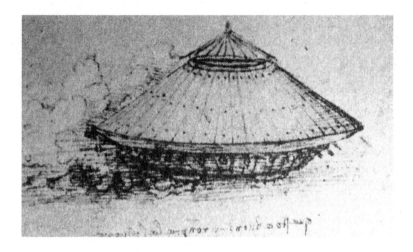

Leonardo da Vinci's tank blueprint (1487)

A tank is an armored vehicle with tracks and weapons.

We can't say when the first armored fighting vehicle was invented.

The Greeks had armored siege engines. In medieval times, horses had a form of armor.

Leonardo da Vinci did some fantastic drawings in 1487 of an armored fighting machine, which many experts say was the prototype of the modern tank.

The vision of Leonardo da Vinci was not built, and the world had to wait until the First World War to see the first tank on the battlefield.

There are apparent differences between the modern tank and that of da Vinci's design, but one thing that they both had in common is that they were intended to frighten the enemy.

The First World War

Little Willy

Until the start of the First World War, the military didn't think there was a place for tanks on the battlefield. There had been ideas for armored vehicles with guns, but the commanders of the armies of Europe and the USA were not interested.

World War One (1914 to 1918) and the coming of trench warfare would soon change military thinking. This new form of warfare would require a new form of weapon.

After a short period of action, the First World War came to a halt as the Germans, the British, and French dug trenches, erected barbed wire, and stopped advancing.

Machine guns guarded the trenches. To take an enemy's trench would mean many casualties. This new form of war was a shock to the military commanders, and something needed to be done to break the stalemate.

Sir Ernest Swinton came up with a design in 1914. Swinton was a British Army officer and engineer who presented his plan for an armored tractor. Sir Winston Churchill, who was the First Lord of the Admiralty, saw the potential.

On September 10, 1915, the first tank in history, Little Willy, was tested.

Little Willy was a British tank:

- Only 1 was produced
- Crew numbered 5
- It weighed 16 tons and had a top speed of 3.5 miles an hour.
- It had armor that was 10 mm thick

Little Willy failed the test, but improvements were made to enable it to cross trenches and crush barbed wire. The new, improved tank was given the rather dull name, the Mark I.

Mass production began, and 150 were made.

The Mark I Tank

The Mark I had a bizarre shape compared to a modern-day tank, with tracks going around the hull. This design, though, solved the problem of crossing ditches and trenches.

A lot of the design features of the Mark I were taken from the navy. The tank had naval guns.

The project was top secret, and to conceal the fact that these were weapons, the government put out a story that they were water storage tanks.

The name stuck.

On September 15, 1916, Mark I tanks got their first taste of action near the River Somme in France.

There were 32 tanks used. Of these, 5 tanks got stuck in the mud, and 9 broke down. The 18 remaining tanks broke through the German lines and went over 3 miles into enemy territory. The British were surprised at how successful the use of tanks had been. It terrified the German soldiers, and fewer British soldiers were killed in the attack.

The Mark I was a British tank.

There were 150 produced

They were equipped with six-pounder guns and Hotchkiss machine guns. They had a crew of 8 people and weighed 28 tons. They were made with 12 mm armor and had a top speed of 3.7 miles an hour.

The German A7V Tank

It didn't take the Germans very long to develop their own tank. The A7V was called the Mobile Fort and was very large.

This was a heavy tank that was used by Germany from March to October, 1918.

Like the British, the German tank was designed to help the infantry break through the enemy trenches.

During the First World War, the ideas about what a tank could be used for were limited to battering through the enemy defenses.

With a crew of 25, this was much bigger than the Mark I tank. The A7V had a top speed of 4 miles an hour, and weighed over 30 tons.

The French Renault FT7

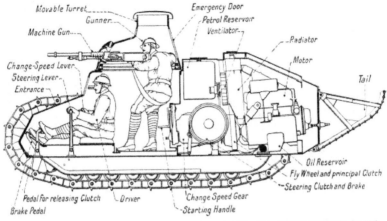

Movable Turret
Gunner
Machine Gun
Change-Speed Lever
Steering Lever
Entrance
Emergency Door
Petrol Reservoir
Ventilator
Radiator
Motor
Tail
Pedal for releasing Clutch
Brake Pedal
Driver
Change Speed Gear
Starting Handle
Oil Reservoir
Fly Wheel and principal Clutch
Steering Clutch and Brake

DIAGRAMMATIC SECTION OF A FRENCH LIGHT (OR "MOSQUITO") TANK.

The inspiration behind the French tank in the First World War was Jean Baptiste Estienne. He wanted a lighter, smaller, and more maneuverable tank than the British and the Germans had produced. He also wanted something cheap to build. He approached the largest French vehicle manufacturer, Louis Renault.

The French tank was different. It only had a crew of 2. There was a driver and a commander who fired the gun. The tank had either a machine gun or a 37mm gun.

The FT7 was the most successful military support vehicle in World War One.

This tank was the first to have its gun inside a rotating turret and was much closer to the modern idea of what a tank should look like.

Jean Baptiste thought that the best way to use tanks in a battle was to have hundreds of them attacking. Thousands of these tanks were ordered, but many were not finished in time and were exported after the war to other countries.

The Renault FT7 was a French light tank. There were 3,950 manufactured. The primary weapon was usually an 8 mm Hotchkiss Machine Gun. There was a crew of 2 people.

This tank weighed just over 7 tons and had a top speed of 4.78 miles an hour. It had 8-16 mm armor.

Blitzkrieg

Many countries became interested in building their own tanks after the First World War. Most military leaders saw the tank as a backup to help troops on the battlefield.

Tanks got heavier before the start of World War Two. No longer were tanks with thin armor considered useful. The reason for this was the Spanish Civil War.

During the Spanish Civil War, it became clear that tanks could be defeated by foot soldiers using field guns and heavy machine guns. These guns could cut through the armor and disable tanks that did not have thick enough armor plating.

The Germans had a theory that they called blitzkrieg (lightning War).

Blitzkrieg was carried out using a lot of tanks traveling in formation. The German idea was that the tank was not on the battlefield to support the infantry (foot soldiers) but to break through enemy lines and cause chaos. The tanks would be fast-moving and heavily armored. Tank units would be fast enough to reach and destroy enemy headquarters situated well beyond the front line.

Tanks would capture the main transport routes and supply depots. The age of static trench warfare was well and truly over by using tanks in this way.

German Military Commanders believed the tank was the most powerful means of attack. All other weapons would be used to support tanks.

The German tank divisions smashed through French defenses in weeks, proving that lightning war did work.

The French had a lot of tanks, but it was the way that these tanks were used that led to them not being effective.

On the Eastern Front, the Germans started using the same Blitzkrieg tactics they had used in France. It all went well, but then they came up against a new generation of Soviet tanks that were heavily armored and had massive firepower.

The Germans became involved in tank battles and developed the Tiger to help them win.

Famous Tanks of World War Two.

The Panzer IV (Germany)

This was a German front-line tank at the start of World War Two. It was similar to the Panzer III. The short 75 mm gun was replaced by a longer barrel to combat the Russian T-34. It was one of the most powerful tanks of World War Two.

Around 8,553 were produced, and this medium tank was fitted with a 7.5 cm gun and 2 MG 34 machine guns. It weighed 20 tons and had a crew of 5. The top speed was 25 miles an hour. It had 50 mm armor.

Tiger I (Germany)

This is probably the most famous of all World War Two German tanks. It had extremely thick armor, a powerful gun, and was massive. It was the sort of vehicle that struck terror into the enemy. It first made an appearance on the Eastern Front in 1942. One shot from its gun could go through 100 mm armor from just over half a mile.

Although a lethal attack vehicle, it was considered unreliable and would catch fire easily. It was used in Russia, North Africa, and the Western Front.

There were 1354 produced. The Tiger had an 8.8 cm gun and two machine guns. It weighed 57 tons and had a crew of 5. It had a top speed of 25 miles an hour and 102mm armor.

T-34 (Russia)

This tank was more than a match for the German Panzer in the Second World War. The T-34 first saw service in 1940. It was renowned for its thick armor, mobility, and firepower. German General von Kleist called it the finest tank in the world.

There were a staggering 57,000 manufactured during World War Two. The T34 had a machine gun and a 76.2 mm gun. The top speed was 33 miles an hour. It weighed 26 tons and had a crew of 4, and 45 mm armor.

The M4 Sherman (USA)

M4 Sherman

This was the most used medium tank by the USA and its allies during World War Two. This tank was reasonably cheap to manufacture and was reliable.

Many of these tanks were given to Russia and Britain in a lend-lease agreement.

The tank was named after William Sherman, the American Civil War General.

There were around 50,000 produced between 1942 and 1945. It had a 75mm main gun and two machine guns.

It weighed 35 tons, and its top speed was 20 miles an hour. The Sherman had 50mm armor and a crew of 4.

M26 Pershing

This tank was used in the final phase of the war against Germany.

Named after General John Pershing (USA), it was seen as a replacement for the Sherman tank.

Delays meant it only played a small part in the war, but it was also used by the USA in the Korean War. It weighed over 40 tons, had a crew of 5 and a top speed of 30 miles an hour.

It used a 90 mm gun and 2 browning machine guns.

Over 2,000 were built during the war years. It had 102 mm armor.

M26 Pershing

The IS-2 (Russia)

This was a Russian heavy tank named after the Russian leader, Joseph Stalin. It was used in World War Two and in other Russian allied countries when the war ended.

This tank was first used in early 1944 in an elite Red Army tank regiment. These tanks were only used for special targets, usually to break through heavily fortified German positions. When the job was completed, other more mobile tanks finished the work.

It was claimed that IS-2 tanks destroyed over 40 German Tiger tanks for the loss of only 8 in operations in Ukraine.

The IS-2 had a crew of 4 and 100 mm sloping armor that would deflect shells. The top speed was 23 miles an hour. About 4,000 of these 40-ton tanks were made during the war, though production carried on after the war was finished. This tank used a D25-T 122 mm gun.

The Jagdpanther (Germany)

This was a German tank destroyer built near the end of the Second World War. This tank had sloped armor and a very modern-looking design. Only 400 were produced, and they were used to destroy enemy tanks, mainly in Russia, though some did see action in Normandy (France).

This tank had a crew of 5 and weighed 46 tons. It used a Pak 43 88 mm anti-tank gun and an MG 34 machine gun.

With a maximum speed of 27 miles an hour and 80 mm sloping armor, this was a formidable weapon but was not enough to stop Germany from being defeated.

Tiger II (Germany)

Nicknamed the King Tiger, the Tiger II was used defensively in the Normandy campaign of 1944.

It was the most powerful tank on the battlefield at the time.

Even though it had limited mobility due to its size, and not many were built, these tanks were devastating at destroying the enemy.

Only 500 were ever produced. Each tank weighed 62 tons.

Its main weapon was the formidable 88 mm KwK43 tank gun backed by 2 MG 34 machine guns.

The Tiger 2 had a crew of 5 and 180 mm armor plating that sloped. It had a top speed of 16 miles an hour.

Panther

The official name of this tank was the PanzerKampfwagen-V-Panther.

It was used by Germany on the western and eastern front from 1943 until the war ended

The Panther is considered the best German tank of the Second World War. It's a fact that the Germans that invaded Russia in June 1941 were taken by surprise at the quality and firepower of the T-34.

The German leader, Hitler, wanted the T-34 to be copied, and the result was the Panther, which went into battle for the first time in Kursk in 1943.

The Panther was bigger and much better quality than the T-34, but German production was slow, and there never were enough Panthers for them to have much of an effect.

Only 3,694 Panthers were made, which is small compared to the Russian T-34.

The main weapon was the 7.5 KwK 42 L/70 cm tank gun backed up by two machine guns. There was a crew of 5.

The top speed was 31 miles an hour, and the armor was 80 mm.

The tank weighed 44 tons.

The Biggest World War Two Tank

Panzer VIII Maus (Germany)

This was going to be the German super-heavy tank. It is the heaviest fully fitted tank ever built. It was completed in late 1944.

Five of these monsters were ordered, but only two hulls and one turret were completed. Russian troops overran the testing grounds.

The tank never saw action. It weighed 188 tons. It had a crew of 6 that were protected by armor 220 mm thick.

The main gun was a 128 mm KWK 44 canon supported by a 75 mm gun.

Hitler wanted the Maus to be a virtually indestructible breakthrough tank.

The Maus would break through enemy lines, and other tanks and troops would follow behind.

Today the Maus is on display at the Kubinka tank museum in Moscow, Russia

Tank Battles of World War Two

Second Battle of El Alamein

British Churchill Tanks during the battle

Tanks played a vital role in the Second World War, but at the beginning of the war, the German blitzkrieg method was most successful.

In North Africa, between 1940 and 1943, the fight in the desert relied on tanks. The British used Matildas, Valentines, and Crusaders, that were lightly armed and broke down a lot. The British benefitted by using American-built Sherman and Grant tanks.

The Second Battle of El Alamein (Egypt) started on October 23, 1942, and finished on November 11, 1942, with a British victory against the German and Italian forces. The victory marked the end of the threat of the invasion of Egypt and led to the Allied forces landing in Italy.

294 German tanks and 298 Italian tanks.

Panzer II, Panzer III, Panzer IV along with Italian Fiat M13/40

1,029 British tanks

Sherman, Grant, and Crusader tanks

500 German tanks destroyed

332-500 British tanks destroyed.

The Battle of Kursk

This was the biggest tank battle ever and took place in Russia between July 5, 1943, and August 23, 1942.

The battle started with a German attack but ended with a Russian counter-attack. On the orders of Hitler, the attack had been delayed and had given the Russians a lot of time to prepare defenses.

This battle was the final major attack of the Germans against Russian forces on Russian soil.

German soldier inspects a knocked-out Russian T-34 during the battle

Russia won the Battle of Kursk even though they lost more soldiers and tanks. However, Russia could replace soldiers and tanks very quickly, but the German Army commanders found themselves fighting on too many fronts. German tactics became defensive as the massive Russian Army attacked and eventually invaded Germany and reaching Berlin.

The Germans used 2,500 tanks and assault guns

The Russians used 3,500 tanks

500 German tanks destroyed

1,500 Russian tanks destroyed

Other World War Two Tanks

Italian

The **P26/40** was a heavy Italian tank used in World War Two. It had a 75 mm gun and a Breda machine gun. Ironically, this tank was not used by Italian forces but by the Germans after the Italians surrendered. The fierce Italian campaign that the German military forces fought ended in defeat.

This tank weighed 26 tons and was operated by a crew of 4. It had a top speed of 25 miles an hour. Only 103 were ever produced.

British

Even though the British did use American Sherman tanks during the war, they did design and build their own.

The **Matilda** had thick armor, but its firepower could not match those of the German tanks. It was slow and was often knocked out by enemy tanks before it was close enough to fire its own gun. However, it was very reliable.

Matilda II in Egypt

The Matilda was operated by a crew of 4 and weighed 27 tons. It had a maximum speed of 16 miles an hour and 78 mm armor.

The early model **Crusader Tanks** were disastrously unreliable and didn't have very heavy armor. Because of their unreliability, more were lost due to engine breakdown than combat. Improvement in armor and guns in the later models proved vital in the Battle of El Alamein and after. The Crusader was later replaced by the more reliable American Sherman and Grant tanks.

Churchill tanks in the desert of North Africa

The **Churchill** had a maximum speed of 15 miles an hour and a crew of 3.

The **Cromwell** tank weighed 27 tons and had a top speed of almost 40 miles an hour.

It had a 75 mm gun and two machine guns, but its main asset was its terrific speed and maneuverability.

The tank was first used in large numbers during the Normandy landings and the campaign to push the German forces out of Northern France.

The German Panzers and Tigers easily outgunned the early Cromwell Tanks, so they had their artillery upgraded to 95 mm howitzers.

Cromwell tanks were used until the end of the war by the British.

The Cromwell had a crew of 5.

Cromwell tank in Normandy, France

France

The **Char B-1** was a French heavy tank created as a breakthrough vehicle. The tank had a 75 mm howitzer in the hull and a turret with a 47 mm gun. It was considered one of the finest tanks of the time and, in confrontation with German tanks, could hold its own.

Low speed and high fuel consumption meant that this tank was not suited to the lightning blitzkrieg war of the Germans. When France was overrun by Germany at the beginning of the war, the German military turned many captured tanks into flamethrowers.

The Char B-1 had a crew of 4 and weighed 28 tonnes. It had a maximum speed of 13 miles an hour.

USA

M3-Lee was an American medium tank that had a turret that was produced in different ways. One for use by the American military

and another for use by the British. Thus, the tank had two names—
Lee for the American turret and Grant for the British.

Even though the M3 had thick armor and good firepower, it had
some design flaws that made its overall performance unsatisfactory.

It was replaced by the Sherman in most theatres of war by the
USA

Even so, the British continued using the tank against the
Japanese, and around 1,000 were supplied to Russia between 1941
and 1943.

With a crew of either 6 or 7, the Ms weighed 30 tonnes and had a top speed of 16 miles an hour. It had 175mm gun in the hull and a 137 mm gun in the turret. The armor was up to 51 mm.

Life Inside a World War Two Tank

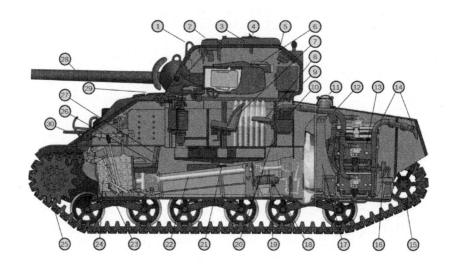

1 ring lift 2 ventilator 3 hatch of the turret 4 periscope 5 turret hatch

6 turret seat 7 gunner's seat 8 turret seat 9 turret 10 air cleaner 11 radiator filler cover

12 air cleaner manifold 13 power unit 14 exhaust pipe 15 track idler 16 water pump

17 radiator 18 generator 19 rear drive shaft 20 turret basket 21 slip ring

22 front drive shaft 23 suspension bogie 24 transmission 25 main drive

26 driver's seat 27 machine gunner/second driver seat 28 gun 29 driver's hatch

30 machine gun

Weighing around 30 tons, the Sherman tank was not the largest or the most powerful in World War Two, but it is one of the most well-known from this era.

This tank made up the backbone of the Allied Army.

What was it like inside? If you had claustrophobia (fear of enclosed spaces), being part of a tank crew wasn't for you.

The tank commander sat on the right side of the turret towards the back. He was in charge of what the tank did and was in direct radio contact with the platoon leader. The tank commander could give directions to the driver by having his head and shoulders out of the turret or using a periscope. The commander usually spent a lot of time with his head and shoulders outside the turret, so he was always a possible target of enemy fire.

The gunner was usually second in command. He sat in front of the commander. He controlled the guns. The guns were fired using a footswitch, and the gunner controlled the rotating turret.

As the name implies, the loader loaded the guns with ammunition for firing. He would also be responsible for fixing the guns if they jammed and also doing maintenance on the guns to keep them running smoothly. The loader sat on the gun's left and had more space and a fold-up seat because of his job.

The driver and co-driver sat in the front of the hull. The driver had to trust the commander telling him what direction he wanted to go in. The commander was the eyes of the driver as his position in the turret gave him all round vision.

With no toilet, no privacy, no beds, and the engine noise, the life of tank crews was not easy, often dangerous, and always smelly.

Thank you for Reading this Book

You can visit the English Reading Tree Page by clicking:

Visit Amazon's Keith Goodman Page (Mailing List)

Books in the Young Learner series

All About the Anglo Saxons

All About the Titanic

All About the Battle of the Little Bighorn

All About the Second World War

All About the American Revolutionary War

All About American History

All About George Washington

All About the Normans

All About Japan

All About Stonehenge

All About Castles

All About the Hundred Years' War

All About World War Two Tanks

Some of the Books in the English Reading Tree Series by Keith Goodman include:

The Titanic for Kids

Shark Facts for Kids

Solar System Facts for Kids

Dinosaur Facts for Kids

American Facts and Trivia for Kids

My Titanic Adventure for Kids

Discovering Ancient Egypt for Kids

Native American Culture for Kids

Meet the Presidents for Kids

The American Civil War Explained for Kids

The American Revolution Explained for Kids

World War One in Brief for Kids

World War Two Explained for Kids

Colonial America for Kids

Middle Ages Facts and Trivia for kids

The Cold War Explained for Kids

The Wild West and Stuff for Kids

The Great Depression and Stuff for Kids

Early American History for Kids

Awesome Alabama for Kids

Twentieth-Century America for Kids

American Democracy Explained for Kids

Amazing Alaska for Kids

America at War for Kids

Titanic Conspiracy Theories for Kids

Famous Americans for Kids

Twentieth Century Heroes and Villains for Kids

Wild West History for Kids

The French Revolution Explained for Kids

Key events that created America

The Bermuda Triangle Mystery for Kids

The Russian Revolution Explained for Kids

UFO Mysteries for Kids

America in the 1970s for Kids

America in the 1980s for Kids

America in the 1940s for Kids

America in the 1990s for Kids

America in the 1930s for Kids

America in the 1920s for Kids

Chinese Dynasties for Kids for Kids

America from 1910 to 1919 for Kids

1917 for Kids

The Titanic Diary for Kids

Myths and Legends for Kids

The Loch Ness Monster for Kids

The Vietnam War for Kids

PzIV.Saumur

Author and licence can be found here

Panzer VI (Tiger I

Author and licence can be found here

T-34

Author and licence can be found here

Jagdpanther

Author and licence can be found here

Tiger II

Author and licence can be found here

Panzer V "Panther

Author and licence can be found here

Author and licence can be found here

M4A4 cutaway

Author and licence can be found here
https://commons.wikimedia.org/wiki/File:M4A4_cutaway.svg

Printed in Great Britain
by Amazon

17148944R00037